It's been 400 years since Shakespeare wrote his last play, yet his stories and characters are as alive today as they were when he first penned them. Students across the world study Shakespeare's plays in school, and they have been translated and performed in almost every language. So, what is it about Shakespeare's work that keeps it relevant through time? Shakespeare's language is rich, his characters are complex and dynamic, and his themes—love, betrayal, honor, bravery, war, politics—are still relevant today.

In this Play On Shakespeare series, we take a lighthearted approach to these classic stories in the hopes of introducing Shakespeare's timeless characters and themes to a new generation of readers.

How to enjoy this book...

Shakespeare's works are not only famous for how entertaining they are and the lessons they teach, but also they are filled with important literary devices. Pay attention to the color of the words as you read along to see what literary device is being used!

GREEN words show SETTING—where the story is taking place.

PURPLE words show the CHARACTERS—who is in the story.

YELLOW words show FORESHADOWING—hints about what is going to come next.

PINK words show SIMILES—comparisons that use the words "like" or "as."

ORANGE words show ALLITERATION—two or more words that start with the same sound.

BLUE words show IMAGERY—descriptive words that can be experienced by one of the five senses.

BOLD BLACK words were invented by SHAKESPEARE and the definitions can be found in the back of the book.

Also note that Shakespeare's plays are separated into "acts," which are the sections of a play, just like chapters are sections of a book. Pay attention to something that happens in each act, and see if you can remember something from each act at the end! For more ideas on how to enjoy this book, please visit FlowerpotPress.com.

Designed by Flowerpot Press
in Franklin, TN.
www.FlowerpotPress.com
Designer: Stephanie Meyers
Editor: Katrine Crow
DJS-0912-0139
ISBN: 978-1-4867-0858-1
Made in China/Fabriqué en Chine

MUCH ADO ABOUT NOTHING

A Play On William Shakespeare's

Adapted by
Luke Daniel Paiva

Illustrated by
Roberto Irace

Kingdome of Scotland

Edinburgh

North Sea

Kingdome of Norway

Goteborg

Kingdome of Sweden

Reign of Denmark

Kingdome of Ireland

Dublin

Kingdome of England

Stratford-upon-Avon

Shakespeare lived here.

London

Netherlands

Hamburg

Berlin

Köln

Saxony

Bohemia

Paris

Kingdome of France

Swiss Conf.

Austria

Verona

Venice

Atlantic Ocean

Toulouse

Savoy

Bilbao

Bar

Naples of N

Porto

Kingdome of Spain

Kingdome of Portugal

Madrid

Valencia

Lisbon

Malaga

Sult. of Fez

of Alg

Mediterranea

Benedick
A loyal friend and comrade of Claudio. He is secretly in love with Beatrice.

Beatrice
The lovely cousin of Hero and niece of Leonato. She is always teasing Benedick, but is secretly in love with him.

Spoiler alert: The play Mu H ADO AB Ut NoTh Ng is known as one of William Shakespeare's comedies, which means that though there may be some trouble during the story, it has a happy ending.

Claudio
A young soldier who is kind, but easily fooled. He is engaged to be married to Hero.

Hero
The beautiful and loving daughter of Leonato. She is engaged to be married to Claudio.

Setting: On the island of Sicily, in the town of Messina, Italy.

Don Pedro
A generous, kind nobleman and longtime friend of Leonato.

Don John
The cranky, jealous half-brother of Don Pedro, who is always stirring up trouble.

Leonato
The respected governor of Messina and Hero's father.

Dogberry
The chief of police, or constable, of Messina. He is very kind and good at his job, but is sometimes hard to understand because he gets his words mixed up.

Margaret
Hero's naive maid, who happens to be madly in love with Borachio.

Borachio
The very mischievous and conniving friend of Don John.

And so our story begins...

Act I

It was a very momentous day on the island of Sicily, in the town of Messina. There was to be a celebration in honor of the brave soldier Claudio and Hero, governor Leonato's daughter. The young couple was in love and engaged to be married.

Claudio and his fellow comrades, Don Pedro and Benedick, had just returned victorious from battle and were riding their steeds among the cheering townspeople, who watched them in **amazement**. They rode through the streets toward Leonato's house to greet the governor, Hero, and their families.

That evening, after the soldiers had arrived, the cheerful celebration began. The party was **majestic**, and the whole town was in attendance, including Hero, Leonato, Hero's cousin Beatrice, and the soldiers.

As our young lovers, Hero and Claudio, reunited,
another romance was brewing between Beatrice
and Claudio's comrade, Benedick.

It was during the fabulous festivities that Don Pedro, the soldiers' fearless leader, realized that Benedick and Beatrice must like each other. Benedick was always stealing adoring glances at Beatrice when she wasn't looking. When Benedick was talking with other people, Beatrice was looking longingly at him.

Don Pedro gathered Hero, Claudio, and Leonato to share with them what he had discovered about their friends. The company agreed that Benedick and Beatrice were in love and they should help unite them. They immediately began working on a plan.

Act II

The plan was simple: whenever Benedick was near, they would discuss how much Beatrice loved him, but was too timid to tell him. Then, they would go near Beatrice and talk loudly about how much Benedick loved her, but couldn't find the words to tell her.

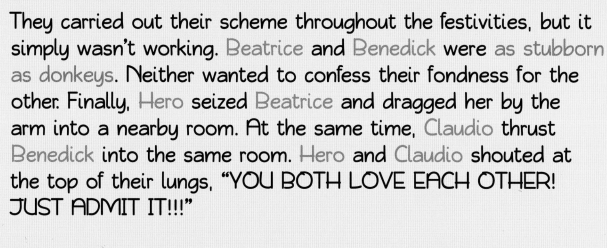

They carried out their scheme throughout the festivities, but it simply wasn't working. Beatrice and Benedick were as stubborn as donkeys. Neither wanted to confess their fondness for the other. Finally, Hero seized Beatrice and dragged her by the arm into a nearby room. At the same time, Claudio thrust Benedick into the same room. Hero and Claudio shouted at the top of their lungs, "YOU BOTH LOVE EACH OTHER! JUST ADMIT IT!!!"

After quite a long period of looking embarrassed and waiting for the other person to **break the ice**, Benedick and Beatrice finally told each other how they felt. Their friends applauded and Benedick and Beatrice began planning their own wedding!

Meanwhile . . .

No one had noticed the very sneaky and ill-tempered Don John, Don Pedro's estranged brother, lurking in the shadows. Don John felt he never received enough attention or celebration for himself. Whenever he went to parties for other people, he would simply sit in the corner and pout. This party wasn't any different, and just to spite everyone there, he began eating the delicious desserts before the rest of the guests had finished dinner. It was at that very moment he overheard his brother's plan to unite Benedick and Beatrice.

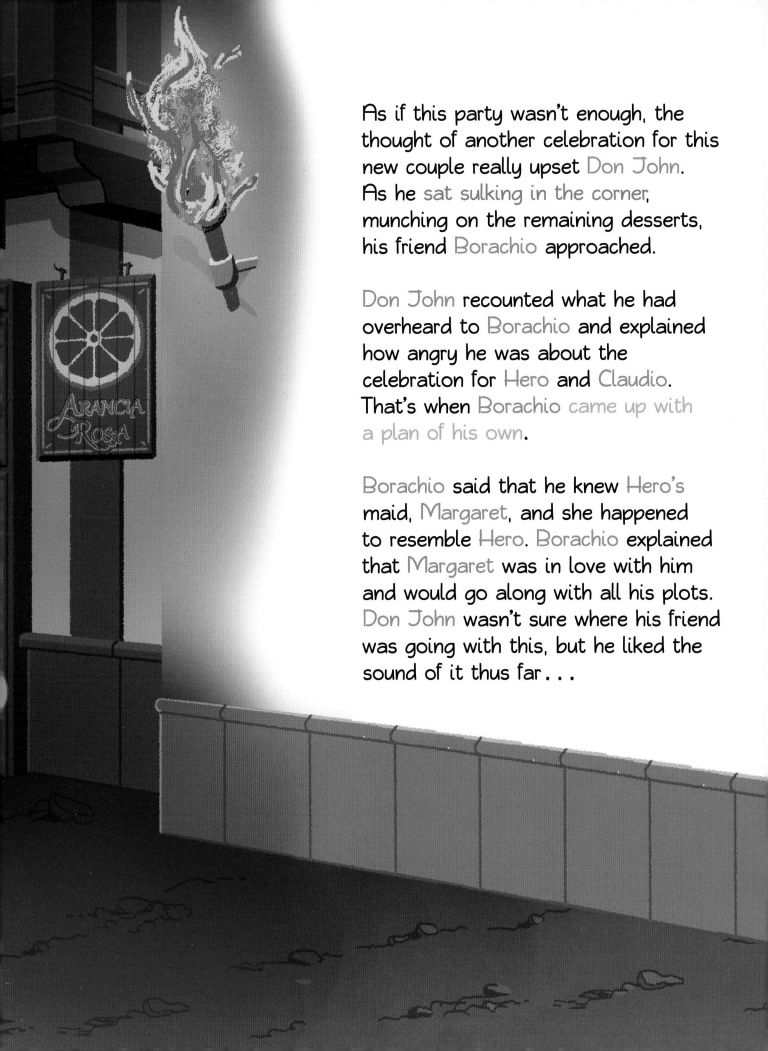

As if this party wasn't enough, the thought of another celebration for this new couple really upset Don John. As he sat sulking in the corner, munching on the remaining desserts, his friend Borachio approached.

Don John recounted what he had overheard to Borachio and explained how angry he was about the celebration for Hero and Claudio. That's when Borachio came up with a plan of his own.

Borachio said that he knew Hero's maid, Margaret, and she happened to resemble Hero. Borachio explained that Margaret was in love with him and would go along with all his plots. Don John wasn't sure where his friend was going with this, but he liked the sound of it thus far. . .

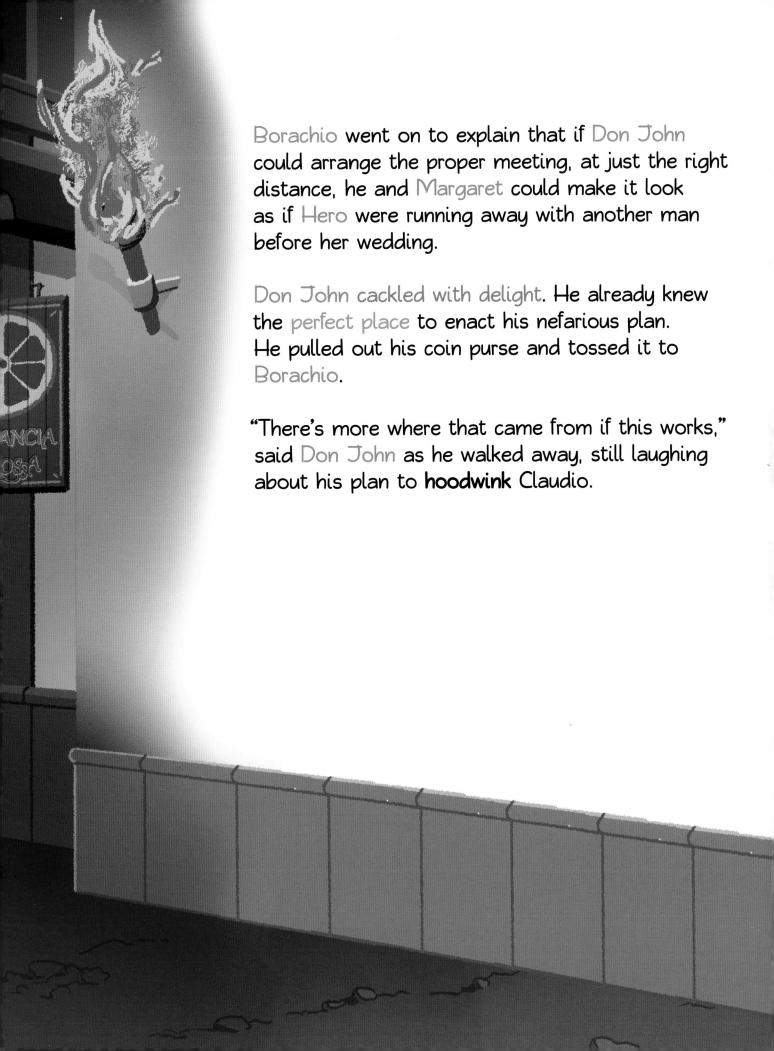

Borachio went on to explain that if Don John could arrange the proper meeting, at just the right distance, he and Margaret could make it look as if Hero were running away with another man before her wedding.

Don John cackled with delight. He already knew the perfect place to enact his nefarious plan. He pulled out his coin purse and tossed it to Borachio.

"There's more where that came from if this works," said Don John as he walked away, still laughing about his plan to **hoodwink** Claudio.

Act III

On the night before the wedding, Don John ran up to Claudio and Benedick, huffing and puffing. He told Claudio that he came bearing dreadful news. He said he had discovered that Hero was in love with another man, and he could prove it if they followed him.

The two men followed Don John to the place he claimed Hero would be and hid behind a bush where they could just barely see Borachio and Margaret in the distance.

Claudio was close enough to hear, but not close enough to see that it wasn't actually Hero.

Claudio heard Margaret say, "I love you."

Then, he heard Borachio say, "I love you, too. We will leave together soon."

Claudio's heart was as broken as shattered glass. He thought his true love was planning to run away with another man.

Act IV

The day of the wedding, Claudio was still devastated. He waited until just before the ceremony to confront Hero in front of all their friends and family. He said he would never marry someone who did not truly love him. Hero was so heartbroken that she fainted.

Benedick, who believed what he had seen the night before, stood by Claudio. And Beatrice, who knew Hero truly loved Claudio and would never do anything to hurt him, tended to Hero.

Benedick and Beatrice each sided with their friend and not with each other, and in the end, they too canceled their wedding.

Everyone in attendance was deeply disappointed for the couples. Everyone that is, except for Don John, the **archvillian**. He was in the back eating a piece of the wedding cake with a sneaky grin upon his face.

Act V

Heroes come in many forms. The hero of this story is not a brave soldier or the wise governor, but Dogberry, the wild-eyed, wild-haired, sloppily dressed, always faithful local constable. The townspeople rarely took him seriously because he mixed up words like "suspect" and "respect," and "comprehend" and "apprehend," but he was an excellent watchdog. He was always looking for people up to no good. That's how he overheard Borachio that night bragging about what he had done. Dogberry arrested Borachio for fraud and made him reveal all the details of Don John's evil plan.

Leonato was overjoyed that his daughter's name had been cleared. Benedick and Beatrice were so thrilled to hear the news that they resumed their wedding planning. But Don Pedro was furious. So furious, in fact, that he ordered his brother be arrested for slander.

Claudio, however, seemed even more upset than before. He felt terrible for embarrassing Hero and hurting her in front of their friends and family. He had found himself **in a real pickle** and couldn't believe he hadn't just trusted Hero from the beginning.

Even Dogberry found it **laughable**. He wanted to know why someone would "enter into the ponds of holly mattress money with someone, and not even suspect their opossum enough to hear their slide of the story."
(He meant to ask why someone would "enter into the bonds of holy matrimony with someone, and not even respect their opinion enough to hear their side of the story," but everyone was used to translating Dogberry and understood what he was saying.)

Thankfully, Hero was a loving and forgiving person. She accepted Claudio's heartfelt apology and reminded him that, in the future, a little honest communication could prevent so much ado about nothing.

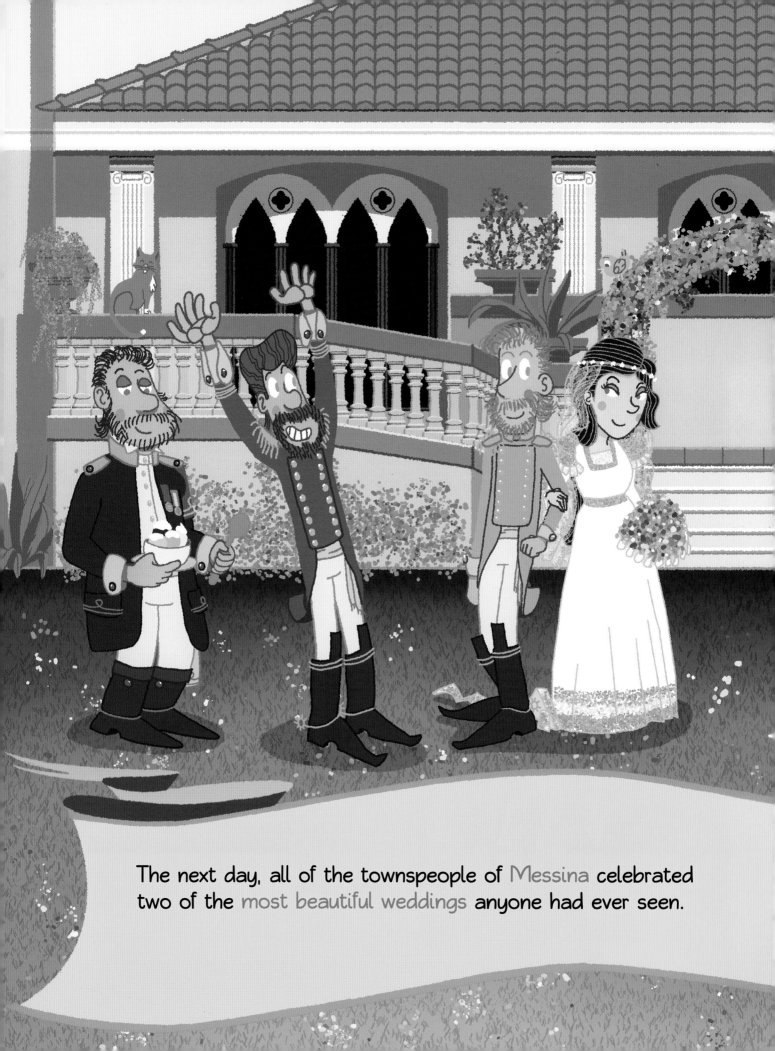

The next day, all of the townspeople of Messina celebrated two of the most beautiful weddings anyone had ever seen.

And with Don John tucked safely away in a jail cell, not a single delectable dessert went missing.

The famous William Shakespeare was born hundreds of years ago, in 1564. He lived in the small market town of Stratford-upon-Avon with his parents, John and Mary, and seven siblings.

Kingdome of Scotland

Kingdome of England

Dublin

Ireland

Stratford-upon-Avon

London

William Shakespeare

At only 18 years old, Shakespeare married Anne Hathaway. They had three children.

In the late 1600s, Shakespeare and friends would have likely pronounced the "Nothing" in MUCH ADO ABOUT NOTHING as "Noting." This was in reference to the amount of noting, or overhearing and observing, that takes place throughout the play. Because of this, the title of the play can be interpreted as a lot of trouble over nothing or a lot of trouble due to eavesdropping!

INK

During his life, Shakespeare wrote 38 plays and 154 sonnets and came up with almost 3,000 words that were added to the English language! He even invented some of the words and phrases we use today, like "bubble," "silliness," and "forever and a day!"

Words and phrases invented by Shakespeare:

Amazement - a strong feeling of surprise or wonder

Laughable - so absurd it is actually funny

Majestic - having or showing impressive beauty or dignity

Hoodwink - to deceive or trick someone

Watchdog - a person or group that keeps an eye out for bad behavior

Archvillain - a principal or extreme villain

"In a pickle" - experiencing a very difficult situation

"Break the ice" - to initiate a conversation

Shakespeare spent much of his career writing works for a company of actors called Lord Chamberlain's Men. He even wrote some of his characters for specific performers in the company. Dogberry was written for an actor named William Kempe, who was known for his hilarious performances.

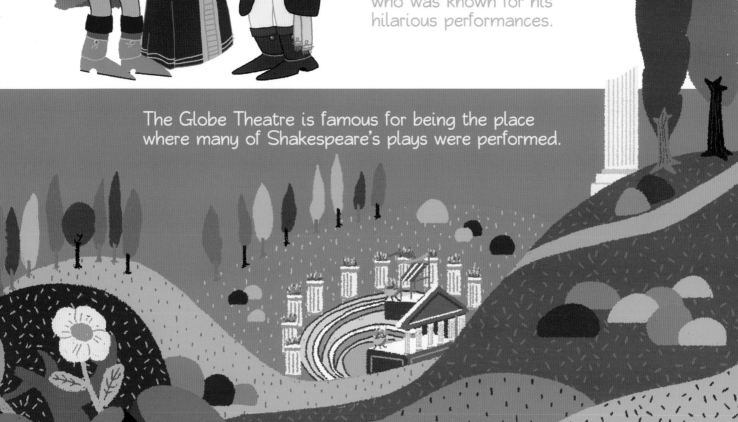

The Globe Theatre is famous for being the place where many of Shakespeare's plays were performed.

To my wife,
for always being there.
—L.P.

To my love, Cristina.
—R.I.